Mrs. Petersen- Personal Copy

The White Cat

retold and illustrated by

ERROL LE CAIN

There was once a king who had three sons. One day he sent for them and said, "My sons, the time has come for one of you to take my place. But first I am going to set you a task. I shall want a dog to keep me company in my old age; whichever of you brings me the cleverest dog in the world will become king."

"Return in a year," the king said, "and bring your dogs with you."

So the three princes set off to look for the cleverest dog in the world, each in a different direction.

The eldest prince sought the advice of the court ladies about finding the world's cleverest dog. They sent him to the city. "You will find many dogs there," they said. The prince soon found that they were right.

The second prince quickly bought a ship so he could search for his dog in distant lands. He learned of a country in which all the dogs could do tricks. So he sailed away to find it and when he arrived he bought every dog in sight.

The youngest prince set off toward the forest. He had heard it was enchanted, and he thought, "Such a forest must be a good place to look for a particularly clever dog."

There he found mice and squirrels and other small creatures. They brushed past him in the darkness; gnarled faces peered at him from the trees. And in a clearing he was startled by the appearance of a strange castle. Its shape was that of a cat.

The prince drew closer to the castle, cautiously crossed the bridge that led to it and, with some hesitation, knocked at the door. It was opened by a cat who was dressed as a footman.

The mistress of the castle came to meet the prince. She was a beautiful white cat, splendidly dressed and followed by her courtiers, all of whom were cats in elegant clothing. The White Cat welcomed the prince and invited him to stay with her.

The prince lingered with the White Cat and was so happy that he forgot the task his father had given him until the year was nearly over.

One day he looked out of the window and saw a huntsman with a dog at his heels. Then he remembered the task and told the White Cat that he must leave at once to go on with his quest.

"Do not be anxious," the White Cat said. "Take this golden egg and go back to your father. When he asks for your dog, open the egg and you shall see what you shall see."

The year was over and crowds gathered around the palace to see the princes return.

The eldest prince went by very fast, for all the dogs he had collected during the year were pulling him.

The second prince had servants to carry his dogs, and the dogs did tricks as they trotted along.

The youngest prince came last, carrying the golden egg.

By the time the youngest prince arrived at the palace, his brothers had presented so many dogs that the king was beginning to wish he had never asked for one. Yet when he saw that his youngest son was carrying nothing but an egg he said severly, "Where is your dog?"

The youngest prince opened the golden egg and to his delight a tiny dog sprang out. The dog danced and juggled, he brought rabbits out of his tiny hat, and finally he bowed to the king.

The king was sure that this must be the cleverest dog in the world, but he was not yet ready to give up his crown. He decided to set his sons a second task.

"Dogs are all very well in their way," he said, "but if you would be a king you will need a queen. Whichever of you can find to be his wife the most beautiful woman in the world shall have my throne. Return in a year with your brides, and please remember," he said to his two older sons, "that you may bring only one wife each."

The eldest prince went back to the city, saw a very pretty girl in a box at the theater, and asked her to marry him. "I might waste a great deal of time," he thought, "without finding anyone more beautiful."

The second prince sailed here and there in his ship till he heard of a country where all the women were remarkably beautiful. He soon found the prettiest of all and persuaded her to marry him.

The youngest prince went directly to the White Cat. Once more, he was so happy with her that he forgot about his task until the year was nearly over.

One day he looked out of the window and saw a girl walking through the forest, and he remembered his quest.

"Do not be anxious," the White Cat said. "I will come back with you to your father and you shall see what you shall see."

Though the prince had grown to love the White Cat dearly, he did not know how he could present her to his father as the most beautiful woman in the world. But he could not bear to say so, and the two of them set off in a coach drawn by a pair of cats. There were two cat footmen in front and two behind. The White Cat sat beside the prince smiling, and said nothing.

Crowds gathered again around the king's palace to see the princes return.

The two elder princes presented their brides to their father. The king welcomed them politely, but the two ladies were equally beautiful and he did not know how to choose between them.

"Where is my youngest son?" the king asked.

At that moment the youngest prince appeared, leading the White Cat. The courtiers looked at her in amazement.

"My son," the king said, "what does this mean? I asked you to bring a beautiful bride and you have brought a white cat. A beautiful cat, I admit, but do you want her to be your wife?"

The prince looked at the White Cat; she only smiled and said nothing. "I know she is a cat, Father," he said, "but I love her and want her to be my wife."

At the prince's words the White Cat put her paws to her face and furled back her fur like a cloak. "An evil fairy cast a spell on me," she said to the prince, "but your love has broken it. Now I am a woman again." And so she was.

"You are the most beautiful woman in the world," the king said, "and now you shall be a queen."

As for the youngest prince, he was so delighted that he could say nothing at all.